Sidney & Norman

a tale of two pigs

Sidney & Norman
a tale of two pigs

written by **Phil Vischer**

illustrated by Justin Gerard

Tommy NELSON®

A Division of Thomas Nelson Publishers
Since 1798

www.thomasnelson.com

jellyfishpress™

SIDNEY & NORMAN: A TALE OF TWO PIGS
Text and art copyright © 2006 by Phil Vischer.
Illustrated by Justin Gerard.
All rights reserved. No portion of this book may be reproduced in any form without the
written permission of the publisher, with the exception of brief excerpts in reviews.
Published in Nashville, Tennessee, by Tommy Nelson®, a Division of Thomas Nelson, Inc.,
in association with Jellyfish™ Labs (http://www.jellyfishland.com), 121 W. Wesley Street,
2nd Floor, Wheaton, IL 60187, and Creative Trust, Inc., Literary Division
(http://www.creativetrust.com), 2105 Elliston Place, Nashville, TN 37203.
Tommy Nelson® books may be purchased in bulk for educational, business,
fund-raising, or sales promotional use. For information, please email
SpecialMarkets@ThomasNelson.com.

Library of Congress Cataloging-in-Publication Data
Vischer, Phil.
  Sidney & Norman : a tale of two pigs / by Phil Vischer ; illustrations by
Justin Gerard.
      p. cm.
  Summary: When oh-so-neat and organized Norman the pig looks down on his
neighbor Sidney, who has trouble managing his messes, an outside force
intervenes and teaches them both a lesson.
  ISBN-13: 978-1-4003-0834-7 (picture book)
  ISBN-10: 1-4003-0834-8
  [1. Neighbors—Fiction. 2. Pigs—Fiction.] I. Gerard, Justin, ill.
II. Title. III. Title: Sidney and Norman.
  PZ7.V8223Sid 2006
  [Fic]—dc22
                                                2006005969

Printed in the United States of America
06 07 08 09 10 WRZ 5 4 3 2 1

To my wife, Lisa

On a quiet street, in a quiet town, lived two pigs.

They didn't oink or eat slop—no, this isn't that kind of story. They wore suit coats and went to work.

And even though they lived right next door to each other, they didn't know each other's names.

The pig on the right was Norman. He was a very good pig. Rules and hard work had always come easily to him, and it showed. His house was neat and organized. He always looked his very best. He gave money to the "needy," and never missed church on Sunday.

Norman's teachers liked him when he was young, and his boss at work liked him now that he was all grown-up. He was pretty sure God liked him, too. After all, he was a very good pig.

Norman figured that everyone could be as good as he
was, if they'd just try a little harder.

He wondered why they didn't.

The pig on the left was Sidney. Things didn't come quite as easily for Sidney. Rules and systems and schedules seemed, well, a bit slippery. One minute he thought he had them, and the next minute—*whoops!* Where'd they go?

He was forever running ten minutes late, and could never manage, no matter how hard he tried, to get his tie perfectly straight. Not like his neighbor . . . what was his name?

Sidney got in trouble in school, which frustrated his teachers. He got in trouble at work, which frustrated his boss.

He knew God was watching, and figured *he* was pretty frustrated, too. But most of all, Sidney frustrated Sidney. Why was everything so hard? Why couldn't he be more like . . . oh, what was his name?

Sidney felt broken. And some days that made it hard to get up in the morning. Some days, in fact, Sidney couldn't get up at all.

Since Sidney was usually late and Norman was usually early, they very seldom saw each other. Unless, that is, they happened to fetch their mail at the same time. Which is exactly what happened one bright morning in October.

Now, normally if Sidney saw Norman, he would look down and shuffle back inside. He was sure Norman was staring at his tie, or his hair, or the papers half-stuck into his briefcase. He was sure Norman was looking down on him for being messy. Which, for the most part, was absolutely correct.

But this day Norman didn't look at Sidney's tie and Sidney didn't look away because they were both staring at the small, pale blue envelopes they had received in the mail. One was addressed to Norman, and the other to Sidney. Hmm. Had someone invited them both to the same party?

Eager to unravel the mystery, the two pigs opened the envelopes. Norman read, "Dear Norman" and Sidney read, "Dear Sidney," followed by: "I would like you to come visit me at 77 Elm Street next Tuesday at your convenience. I have something to tell you."

They both glanced at the bottom of the page and read: "Sincerely, God."

Sidney and Norman reread the invitations several times to make sure they had read them correctly. *God* wanted to talk to them? On *Tuesday?* On *Elm Street?*

Sidney panicked. Deep in his heart was a familiar feeling—the feeling he had felt when, as a young pig, his teacher had sent him to the principal's office. Terror. Panic. Doom.

Norman smiled. He, too, felt a familiar feeling—the feeling he had felt when, as a young pig, he was called up in front of the school to receive an award. Anticipation. Happiness. Pride.

Sidney taped the invitation to the inside of his front
door so he wouldn't lose it. Norman entered the date
neatly in his datebook.

Both pigs had trouble sleeping that night, for very different reasons.

Tuesday came. Norman awoke early, dressed, and headed down the street with the pale blue envelope firmly in hand. Just waking up, Sidney saw him pass by the window and rushed for the shower.

Norman walked tall and proud. Others on the street noticed he looked a bit taller—and more than a little puffier—than usual that morning. His hair was neat and his tie extraordinarily straight. Much straighter than anyone else's on the street! God would certainly be pleased.

Norman found the address and went inside, greeting the woman at the front desk with his "important" voice. She directed him down a long hall, through a heavy wooden door and into a large room, where he found God sitting behind an immense desk. The sight made Norman nervous. But then, he thought, what did he have to be nervous about? He was a good pig.

God walked around the desk and smiled at the puffed-up pig. "I'm glad you could make it," he said warmly. "I have a few things to tell you."

"First of all," God began, "I love you." Norman smiled, though he wasn't surprised.

"Secondly, your *goodness* is not the reason I love you." Norman startled a little. What a curious thing for God to say.

"Thirdly," God continued, "you're not as good as you have led yourself to believe. You're prideful. You're selfish. You look down on others, simply because things don't come as easily for them."

God looked a little sad now. "I love them just as much as I love you. Don't look down on those I love."

Then God smiled and returned to his desk. "That is what I needed to tell you."

Norman swallowed hard. *That* was the award? *That* was the commendation? Confused, he turned and ran down the hall, past the front desk, and back out onto the street. His head was spinning. He felt dizzy. Was God finding fault with *him*?!? He was a *good* pig!

He noticed his tie was off-kilter, and hurried to straighten it. Not perfect, but at least better than that fellow over there in the yellow jacket. Or the guy in the blue. Or *any* of these people, for that matter!

Then it hit him: He was looking down on those people. Right then! Right there! Just like God had said! And he'd done it yesterday—and the day before! Twenty times a day at least! Norman's face grew hot. God was right! He *was* selfish! He *was* prideful!

For the first time in his life, the good pig had to face the fact that he had been very, very bad. His pride in his "goodness" was his sin! He buried his face in his hands and hurried home, tears splashing on his neat gray suit.

From his window, Sidney saw his neighbor return—
and froze in shock. Was he *crying?* Sidney couldn't
breathe. *Oh, dear. Oh, dear.* If that's what a visit with
God did to *that* guy . . . oh! He was doomed!

Hands shaking, Sidney tried one more time to get
his tie to lie just right. Why was it so hard?!? Now,
where was his hat? Not on the hook, of course. Oh,
under the couch. Hat in hand, he peeled the pale blue
envelope off the door and stepped outside.

A bird was singing that morning, but Sidney didn't hear it. The sun was shining brightly, but Sidney didn't see it. *Doomed*, he thought. *Doomed*.

Sidney trudged down the sidewalk, and suddenly was back in school. A little pig, headed down the long hall toward the principal's office. Hands sweating. Heart racing.

Doomed.

He'll see right through me, Sidney thought as he turned onto Elm Street. *My messes, my mistakes—everything.* And then he was there. Though he had walked as slowly as he could, he was there.

Sidney stepped inside. He tried to say something to the woman at the front desk, but found he couldn't speak. She smiled and motioned him to a heavy wooden door down the hall. He gulped.

A few moments later he stood before the door. He wanted to run away. He wanted to hide. But there was no place to go, and nothing to hide behind. So, hat in hand, he pushed open the door and slipped inside. And there, behind the desk, was God.

Sidney gulped again.

"I'm glad you could come," God said, smiling. Sidney tried to respond, but couldn't make a noise.

"I want to tell you something," God continued as he came around the desk. Sidney glanced around nervously. Maybe if he apologized—

"First of all," God began, "I love you."

Sidney startled—surprised.

"Secondly," God continued in a quieter voice, "I love you."

Sidney was gripping his hat a little less tightly now.

"And thirdly . . ." God paused, very close to Sidney. "I love you."

The look in God's eyes warmed Sidney right down to his toes. "That is what I wanted to tell you," God said as he stepped back toward his desk, still smiling.

Sidney stood frozen for a moment; then, realizing God had finished, he turned and ran quickly from the room.

"I don't understand," he said aloud when he reached the street. "Didn't he see me? Didn't he see who I am?" It didn't make sense. Then it occurred to Sidney—"I did it! I fooled him!" Sidney looked at the others on the street, smiling. "Yes, that must be it! I looked good when it was most important—and he bought it!"

Just then Sidney caught his reflection in a store window. His hair was rumpled. His tie, off-kilter as usual, sported a large toothpaste stain. His smile vanished. That couldn't be it. He couldn't have fooled anybody—not looking like that.

Sidney was confused. There was only one other possibility—that God . . . just . . . loved him. Exactly like he was. Messes and all. Sidney felt the warmth he had seen in God's eyes welling up inside him again.

Others on the street would later talk about the small, messy pig they saw that day that appeared to be, well, glowing. All the way home Sidney looked for words to tell everyone what he was feeling, but all he found were tears. Happy tears. Lots of them.

The next day, two pigs emerged from their homes on a bright, crisp October morning and looked at each other. The pig on the left, named Sidney, who seemed a bit taller than before, looked at his neighbor's neat, straight tie and clean clothes—and smiled.

The pig on the right, named Norman, who seemed ever so slightly less "puffy," looked at his neighbor's crooked tie and rumpled hair—and smiled. It was a real smile, too. The kind that comes from deep inside. The kind he hadn't smiled in a long, long time.

Sidney and Norman became good friends. There were still mornings now and then when Norman would wake up feeling a little "puffy." But all he had to do was remember what he had learned at 77 Elm Street. Then the puffiness would quickly vanish, and his real smile would return.

And as for Sidney, he still had his share of messes, though not as many as before. And there were still a few days when he wasn't quite sure he could get up in the morning.

But if you stood outside his window on one of those days, this is what you'd hear:

"First of all, he loves me.

Secondly, he loves me.

And thirdly—

He loves me."

And that was all it took.

About This Book

I wrote this story to try to communicate a simple truth I've noticed over the last few years: It seems that some people need to be reminded that they fall short of God's standards— need their consciences pricked, if you will—and some people really, really don't.

I'm a Norman. Following rules has always come fairly easy to me, and as a result, I've always come across as a good kid. Teachers liked me. Church leaders liked me. Being good, or at least looking good, was never much of a challenge. Behaviors that got me praised, I adopted. Behaviors that got me in trouble, I avoided. It really wasn't that hard. As a result, I don't think I ever really struggled with the notion that God loved me. In fact, if I had been perfectly honest, somewhere down deep I probably thought that I deserved it.

My wife, Lisa, on the other hand, is a Sidney. Rules, structures, systems—they were all a bit slippery. She wanted to look like a good kid, but deep down inside knew that it was just an act. A bluff. A deception. She knew who she really was, and desperately wanted to avoid the humiliation of others finding out.

And then she married me! I saw her messes and struggles, and decided it was my duty as "God's messenger" to point them all out to her, so she could work on them. Which I did. And though she tried, the more I pointed out her shortcomings and the more she failed to quickly and neatly correct them, the more broken and ashamed she felt. And some days, she wasn't sure she could get up at all.

Into this mess, we both needed to hear God's truth. But the truths we needed were as different as we were. I needed to hear God say, "You arrogant, self-righteous windbag! Do you really think you're living up to my standard?" Which I did, in the form of the Holy Spirit's conviction about my relationship with Lisa and others, as well as numerous Scripture passages on holiness and God's standards.

I was so broken when God allowed me to see my arrogance and its impact on those around me that I could do nothing but weep.

As for Lisa, she didn't need to be reminded that she was falling short of God's standard. She'd been reminding herself of that every day of her life. What she needed was to fall into God's arms and hear him say, "First of all, I love you. Secondly, I love you. And thirdly, I love you. Messes and all."

I've got some shocking news for you: There are no "good pigs." I've met a lot of Normans, and I've met a lot of Sidneys, and I'm here to tell you we're all broken. The fact that some of us have become pretty adept at hiding it only makes matters worse for all of us, frankly. So if you're a Norman like me, drop the charade. You can fool some of the people all of the time and all of the people some of the time, but you can't fool God any of the time. Ask God to show you your sin and to "create a new heart" in you sensitive to all of God's commands, not just those that make you look good or bad in public. And come clean with the Sidneys in your life. Believe me, the good pig routine isn't doing them any favors.

If you're a Sidney, ask God to help you quiet the voices of shame and despair and replace them with God's own still, small voice, whispering, "I love you. I love you. I love you." And read the works of folks like Brennan Manning who are as familiar with the path away from self-hatred as I am with the path away from self-righteous windbag.

"While we were yet sinners, Christ died for us." That's the beauty of the Gospel. We're all broken. We're all messed-up pigs. When we can accept that, we're ready to become the new creations God intended us to be. And that's when the fun starts!

–Phil

Using This Book with Kids

While on the surface a book about two pigs in business suits may not seem particularly applicable to kids, I think this one is. While the kids in your life may not be conscious of the issues addressed in this book, the reality is they're immersed in them every day at school, at church, on their sports teams. Awards and accolades tend to gravitate toward certain kids and away from others. The messages our kids receive from teachers, coaches—and even, with the best intentions, from us—can push them toward pride or despair . . . toward self-righteousness or self-hatred.

So what do we do? Point out to our kids the simple truth of this story: God didn't love Norman any more because of his awards and accolades . . . and he didn't love Sidney any less because of his messes. God's love is completely unaffected by what we do—he just loves us. The message of this book for kids is that, regardless of whether your life is filled with awards or detentions, straight-As or Ds, God loves you just the same. So much so, in fact, that he died for you, and would do it again in a heartbeat.

As for us grownups, we need to work hard to show our kids that their value isn't determined by their performance. Never connect your love for your child with what they have just done—or failed to do. As much as we may admire the success of our little Normans, their lives will become miserable if they believe each new test of their abilities holds the power to render them worthless. Unlovable. If success comes easily to your child, make sure they know they're loved for who they are, not what they do. Make sure they know they're precious even when they've done nothing at all. And point out how Norman's natural abilities made it easy for him to look down on those less gifted. Ability—without humility—can become very ugly, indeed.

As for those kids who find life a struggle, those more likely to lose their homework than ace it, those inevitably picked last at recess, just love them. Sure, help them develop their weak areas and identify their own unique strengths, but above all else, never link your love or acceptance to their performance. (And don't label your kids Sidney or Norman, as tempting as it might be.

All kids naturally have their Sidney and Norman areas, and labels applied at an early age can become self-fulfilling prophecies.) Instead, start and end their days by saying, "First of all, I love you. Secondly, I love you. And thirdly, I love you." Even on their very, very bad days. Especially on their very, very bad days.

As they grow, our kids will find it much easier to see the unconditional love in God's eyes—if they've already seen it in ours.

–Phil